Ages 6–7

LEVEL 1

How to Read and Understand

LEARNING WORKBOOK

© 2014 Disney Enterprises, Inc. All rights reserved.

Published by Scholastic Australia in 2014.

Scholastic Australia Pty Limited
PO Box 579 Gosford NSW 2250
ABN 11 000 614 577
www.scholastic.com.au

Part of the Scholastic Group
Sydney • Auckland • New York • Toronto • London • Mexico City
• New Delhi • Hong Kong • Buenos Aires • Puerto Rico

ISBN 978-1-74362-958-1

Printed in China by RR Donnelley.

Scholastic Australia's policy, in association with RR Donnelley, is to use papers that are renewable and made efficiently from wood grown in sustainable forests, so as to minimise its environmental footprint.

10 9 8 7 6 5 4 3 2   14 15 16 17 18 / 1

Welcome to the Disney Learning Program!

The **Disney Learning Workbooks** are the perfect tools to make a difference in your child's learning. Inside this book, you'll find a developmental progression of activities specifically designed to help your child master essential skills critical for learning success. Interactive stickers, puppets and easy-to-read mini books motivate your child to read and understand all sorts of stories!

Children learn to read at different rates, and it takes time and practice. Reading is an active process, so it's important that we learn how to understand what we read. Confident readers understand, remember and talk about what they read. They use a variety of strategies to make sense of what they are reading, such as:

- predicting what might happen next,

- noting important details in the text,

- asking and answering questions about what was read,

- making connections with their own experiences.

We believe that children should have opportunities to read all kinds of books every day to put their developing comprehension strategies to work. The Disney Learning Workbooks are carefully graded to present new challenges to developing readers. They are filled with familiar and fun characters from the wonderful world of Disney to make the learning experience comfortable, positive and enjoyable. Your child will be eager to pick up a book on their own to read more!

As partners in education with the Disney Learning Workbooks, you can help your child reach important milestones in the journey to becoming a confident and independent learner.

Thank you for choosing the Disney Learning Program to support your young learner!

Louise Park
M.Ed. (Children's Literature and Literacy)
Project Consultant

In this book, you will practise looking for important details about characters, where a story takes place and what the main idea in the story might be. You'll also find lots of real-life and make-believe stories to read on your own to help you become a stronger reader.

As you read a story, think about what might happen next. Look for clues and then make a prediction. Read on to see if it happens.

Try retelling a story to help you remember what happens. After you read, stop and think about what took place in the beginning, middle and end of the story.

Details are important. They can help you learn more about characters, settings and more.

Talk about the books you've read with your friends! What surprised you? What made you laugh? What new things did you learn?

Don't forget to use what you know to think about what you are reading. **This helps you understand what you are reading.**

True stories with real-life characters are called **nonfiction**. Stories with make-believe characters are called **fiction**.

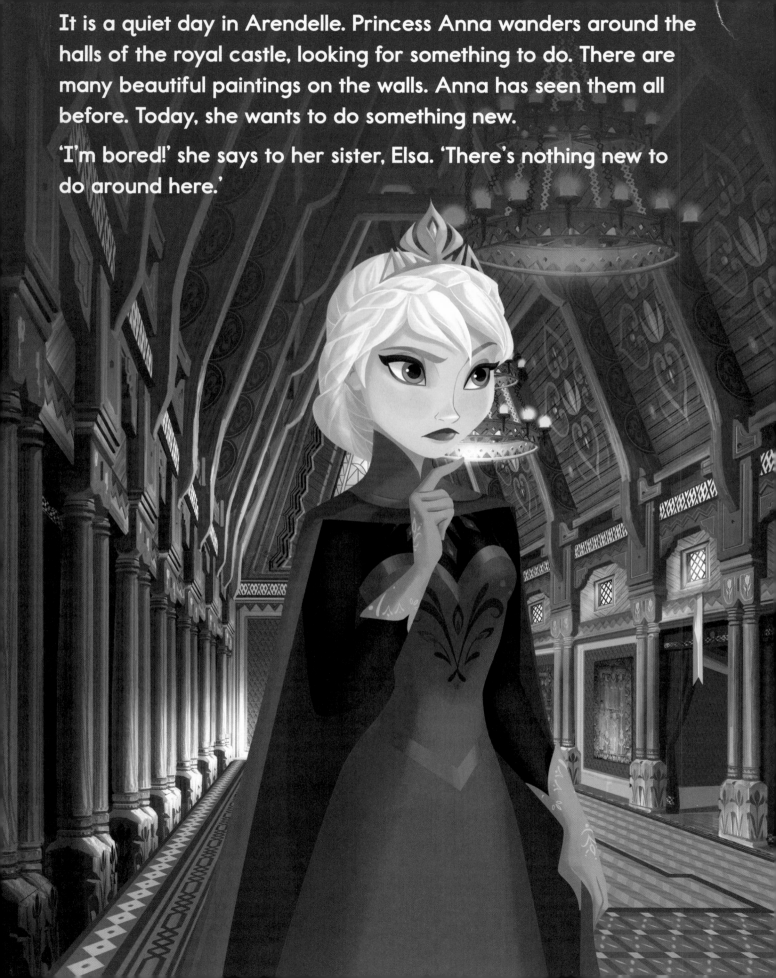

It is a quiet day in Arendelle. Princess Anna wanders around the halls of the royal castle, looking for something to do. There are many beautiful paintings on the walls. Anna has seen them all before. Today, she wants to do something new.

'I'm bored!' she says to her sister, Elsa. 'There's nothing new to do around here.'

Elsa looks at her little sister. Anna is always looking for fun things to do outdoors. But maybe she doesn't know that there are lots of fun things to do indoors as well.

'Why don't you try reading a book?' Elsa suggests. 'The castle library is filled with so many great books. I'm sure we can find one you'll like.'

Anna laughs. 'I don't know why I didn't think of that,' she says.

Elsa smiles. 'Let's go to the library. We will find the perfect story for you.'

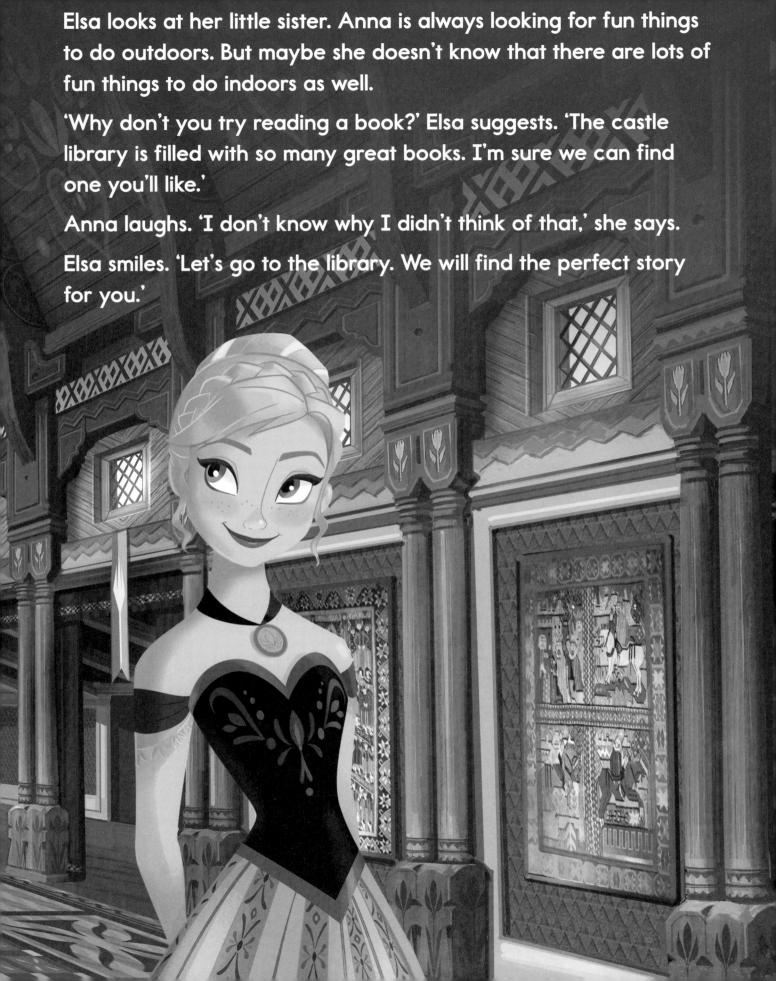

Here is a story about a family activity.

Snowballs

Anna and Elsa are in the castle. Elsa has made it snow inside! They are having a snowball fight. It is great fun. Olaf comes into the castle.

'Hello, friends!' he says. 'What are you doing?'

Anna grins. 'We are having a snowball fight,' she says. 'I am winning!'

Elsa giggles. 'I wouldn't be so sure about that!' She grabs three snowballs and throws them at her sister. Olaf catches one of them.

'Hey!' he says. 'I have a snowball now, too. Can I join in?'

Let's Understand

Read the questions about *Snowballs.*
Put an ✗ next to the correct answer.

1. **What are Anna and Elsa doing?**

   ☐ cleaning the castle

   ☐ building snowmen

   ☐ having a snowball fight

2. **How many snowballs does Elsa throw at Anna?**

   ☐ one

   ☐ two

   ☐ three

3. **What do you think will happen next?**

   ☐ Olaf will join in the game.

   ☐ The sun will come out.

   ☐ Anna will eat a cookie.

Think about the story **Snowballs.** Answer the questions by drawing a picture in each box. Label the pictures.

Who is this story about?

Where does the story take place?

Let's Write

Draw a picture of yourself having fun in the snow.
Write a sentence that goes with your picture.

Read the question. Write the word from the box that answers the question. Find the matching stickers.

grabs   **grins**   **giggles**

1. **What word from the story means <u>smiles</u>?**

_____

- -

_____

2. **What word from the story means <u>laughs</u>?**

_____

- -

_____

3. **What word from the story means <u>takes</u>?**

_____

- -

_____

Here's another story about friends.

Sven and Olaf

Sven and Olaf went flying in hot air balloons. They were high up in the air.

'Can you see the mountains over there, Sven?' Olaf asked. Sven nodded.

'I can see the castle over here!' said Olaf.

The friends had fun on their big adventure.

1. Circle the character names in the story above.

2. Draw a line under the place where the story takes place.

3. What can Sven and Olaf see from the balloon?

   _____

   Sven can see _____.

   _____

   Olaf can see _____.

4. What things can you see around you?

   _____

   I can see _____.

This is a true story about horses.

Horses

Horses are four-legged animals. They eat plants like grass and can run very fast. Horses can run only a few hours after they are born.

Humans have worked with horses for thousands of years. We can ride horses. They can also pull carts and wagons. They are very useful animals.

Horses live on farms and also in the wild. They like to live in large groups called herds.

Let's Write

Draw a picture of one thing you learned about horses.
Write a sentence that goes with your picture.

Let's read about Sven.

Sven Can Skate!

Sven is at the frozen lake. It's time to skate. Oh, no! Sven does not know how to skate! Sven is sad.

'I'll teach you,' says Olaf. They go to the lake. 'Put your feet on the ice,' says Olaf. 'Now, push them forwards slowly.'

Sven tries to skate all day. He slips and slides everywhere. At last, he glides over the ice. Olaf glides next to him. 'Sven, you can skate!' Olaf cries.

Oh dear! Sven and Olaf glide right into a pile of snow!

'Now let's learn how to stop!' Olaf says. The friends laugh together.

Let's Understand

Read the questions about *Sven Can Skate!*
Put an ✖ next to the correct answer.

1. **Where is Sven?**

   ☐ at school

   ☐ at the lake

   ☐ at a friend's house

2. **How does Sven feel at first?**

   ☐ excited

   ☐ happy

   ☐ upset

3. **Why do Sven and Olaf laugh at the end of the story?**

   ☐ Sven can skate, but he can't stop.

   ☐ Olaf makes a joke.

   ☐ It's time for lunch.

Write what happens at the beginning,
middle, and end of *Sven Can Skate!*

Beginning

_____

Sven cannot _____ .

↓

Middle

_____

Olaf _____ him how to skate.

↓

End

_____

Sven finally _____ on the ice.

Let's Write

Draw a picture of yourself doing something fun.
Write a sentence that goes with your picture.

Let's Learn Antonyms

Some words have opposite meanings.
Words that have opposite meanings are called **antonyms**.
Happy and sad are **antonyms**.
Use a word from the box to write the **antonym**.
Find the matching stickers.

under	cold	night

1. **hot**

   _____

   - - - - - - - - - - - - - - - - - - -

   _____

2. **over**

   _____

   - - - - - - - - - - - - - - - - - - -

   _____

3. **day**

   _____

   - - - - - - - - - - - - - - - - - - -

   _____

Let's Retell the Story

Carefully cut out the pictures on the dotted pink lines.
Fold along the blue lines so the pictures will stand up.
Use the pictures to retell *Sven Can Skate!*

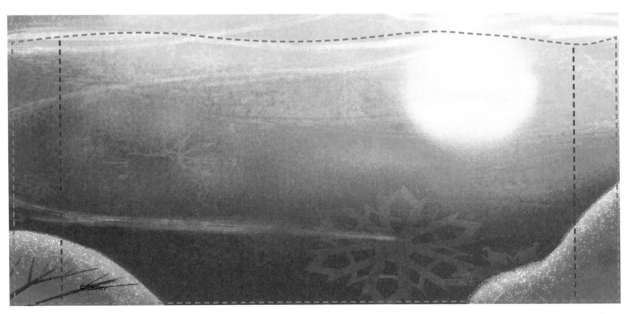

Draw a picture of yourself learning something new.
Write a sentence that goes with your picture.

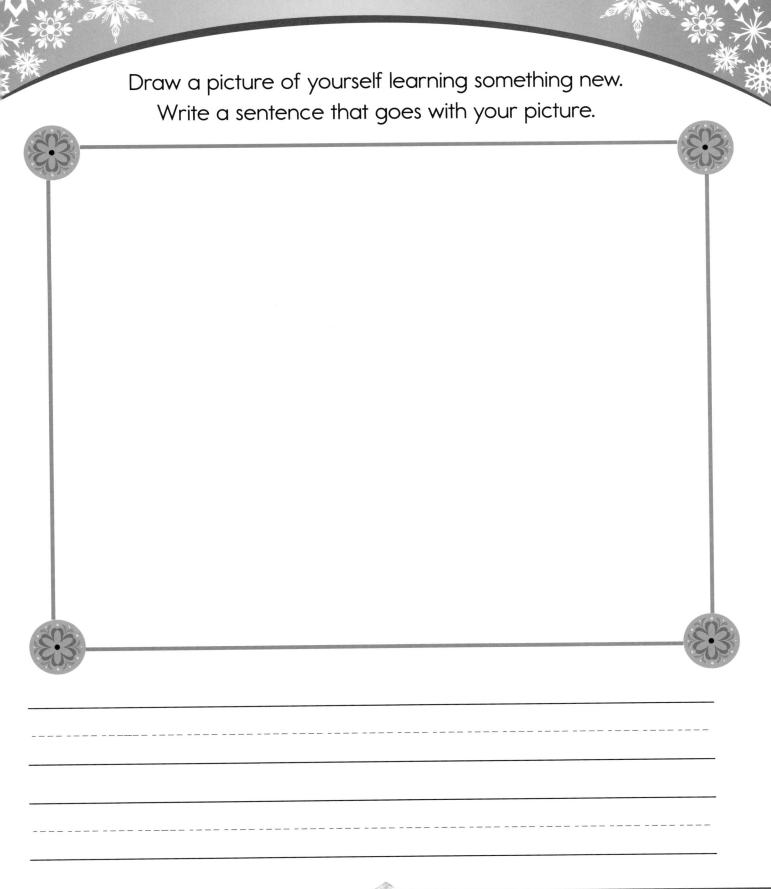

Let's read about a new friend.

A New Reindeer Friend

Anna, Elsa and Olaf went up to the snowy mountains for a picnic. They saw a baby reindeer. He was stuck on a cliff!

'I can help!' said Elsa. She made a ramp out of ice. 'Climb up the ramp,' she told the reindeer. But the reindeer slipped on the ice and could not climb it.

'I can help!' said Anna. She slid down the ramp holding some rope. She tied the rope around the reindeer. 'Pull him up,' she told Elsa and Olaf.

Soon the baby reindeer was safe and sound with his new friends!

Let's Understand

Read the questions about *A New Reindeer Friend.*
Put an ✗ next to the correct answer.

---

1. Where did Anna and Elsa go?

☐ to the shops

☐ to the moon

☐ to the mountains

---

2. What did they find?

☐ a baby reindeer

☐ a snowman

☐ cookies

---

3. Who pulled the reindeer to safety?

☐ Anna

☐ Elsa and Olaf

☐ Sven

Find the stickers for *A New Reindeer Friend.*
Put them in the right order.
Use the stickers to retell the story.

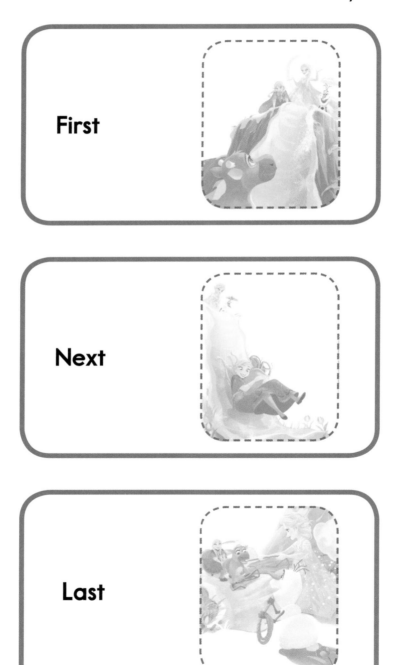

First

Next

Last

Let's Write

Draw a picture of yourself making new friends.
Write a sentence that goes with your picture.

Let's Learn Synonyms

Some words mean the same thing.
Words that mean the same thing are called **synonyms.**
Big and large are **synonyms.**
Use a word from the box to write the **synonym.**
Find the matching stickers.

afraid   glad   angry

1. mad

   _____

   -

   _____

2. scared

   _____

   -

   _____

3. happy

   _____

   -

   _____

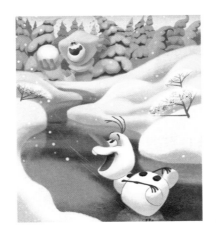

Happy Marshmallow

Marshmallow is feeling grumpy. Olaf is going to cheer him up!

First, Olaf throws a snowball at Marshmallow. Marshmallow is surprised! He plays tag with Olaf.

It is time to go home. Marshmallow and Olaf skate down the frozen river back to the castle. They are just in time for hot chocolate!

Write 1, 2, 3, 4 to show the order of these events.

_____ They drink hot chocolate.

_____ Olaf throws a snowball.

_____ It is time to go home.

_____ Marshmallow and Olaf play tag.

Here's a true story about boats.

Boats

Boats are a way for people to travel across water. There are many types of boats. Very big boats are known as ships. People have been using ships to travel for thousands of years.

Ships can have big sails. They are big sheets of stiff cloth. When the wind blows, it pushes against the sails. This moves the ship forward.

The front of a ship is called the prow. Sometimes the prow is shaped like a person or an animal. The back of a ship is called the stern. A ship's flag is flown from the stern.

A ship is made of many parts. Look at the diagram.
Answer the questions.

prow — sails — stern

1. What does the diagram show you?

_____

- -

_____

2. Where is the ship's flag?

_____

- -

_____

3. What is the wind pushing against?

_____

- -

_____

Arendelle Castle is in a make-believe place. But there are lots of castles in real life that you can visit.

Kronborg Castle

Kronborg Castle is in Denmark. It is a very big castle. It is also very old.

Kronborg Castle was built by King Eric of Denmark in the year 1420. That's nearly six hundred years ago! The castle is built out of stone. It was built on an island between Denmark and Sweden. Two hundred years after it was built, there was a big fire at the castle. King Christian of Denmark fixed the parts of the castle that had burned. The castle has a high wall all around it, many towers and a big rectangular courtyard.

Many kings lived at Kronborg Castle over hundreds of years. Today, it is a museum for visitors. People travel from all over the world to see the beautiful castle and all the treasures inside.

Read the questions about **Kronborg Castle.**
Put an **✗** next to the correct answer.

1. **Kronborg Castle is _____.**

   ☐ very old

   ☐ make-believe

   ☐ very new

2. **The castle is built out of _____.**

   ☐ cake and chips

   ☐ stone

   ☐ bricks

3. **The castle was once damaged by _____.**

   ☐ an earthquake

   ☐ a storm

   ☐ a fire

4. **Today, Kronborg Castle is _____.**

   ☐ a museum

   ☐ where the King of Denmark lives

   ☐ no longer standing

Think about the story **Kronborg Castle.**
Complete the sentences.
Draw a picture to go with each sentence.

The castle has many _____ .

There is a high _____ around the castle.

Let's Write

Draw a picture of a real or make-believe castle you would like to visit. Write a sentence about your picture.

Draw a line to match words that are **antonyms.**

hot	day
sad	cold
over	happy
night	under

Draw a line to match words that are **synonyms.**

afraid	angry
mad	scared
glad	chilly
cold	happy

The Bees and the Coconut

Olaf was on a sunny holiday. He had a nap under a big coconut tree. When he woke up, he saw a big, shiny coconut high up in the tree.

'I want to pick that coconut for Queen Elsa.' He climbed up the tree trunk. He twisted the coconut in his hands. POP! Off came the coconut. Then he heard a buzzing noise. It was coming from the coconut!

'Oh dear!' said Olaf. 'It was not a coconut at all. It was a beehive!' The bees came out of the hive. They flew around Olaf's head. They sat on his nose.

'It's lucky I'm not afraid of bees,' Olaf said. 'They can't sting my carrot nose. But I will put the hive back into the tree. I can find another coconut to give to Queen Elsa!'

What did Olaf do?

_____

_____

What happened?

_____

_____

Let's Write

Draw a picture of something you are afraid of.
Write a sentence that goes with your picture.

ANNA'S ICY ADVENTURE

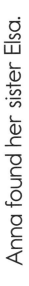

Anna met Sven and Kristoff on a cold night.

She was looking for her sister.

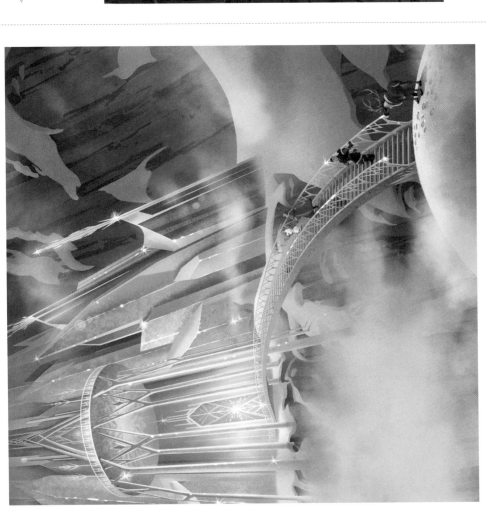

Anna found her sister Elsa.

She lived in a pretty ice palace!

Sven and Kristoff helped Anna.

They travelled across the snow.

The snow was so pretty!

They met a snowman.

His name was Olaf.

3

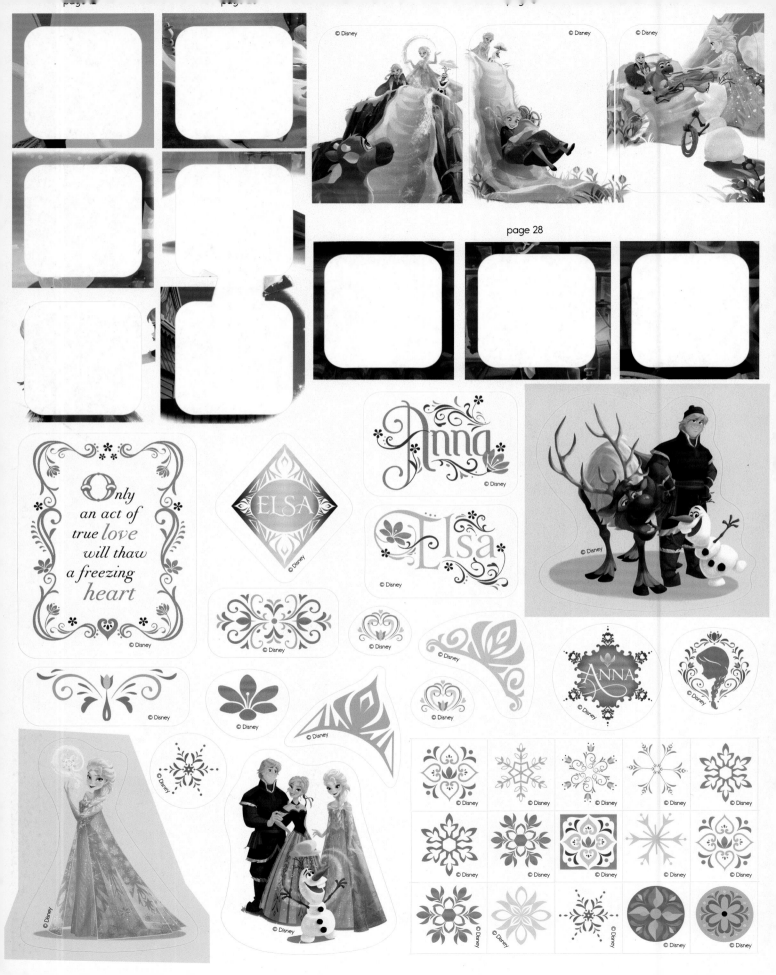

page 28

Only
an act of
true *love*
will thaw
a freezing
heart

© Disney

Anna

ELSA

Elsa

Anna

page 56

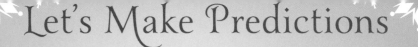

Let's Make Predictions

Anna is going to read *The Northern Lights.*

What do you think *The Northern Lights* will be about?

_____

- -

_____

_____

- -

_____

Put an ✖ next to one thing you might learn about in *The Northern Lights.*

☐ Santa Claus

☐ lights in the northern sky

☐ a shop that sells lights

☐ stars

Now, let's read to find out!

The Northern Lights

When you look up at the night sky, you see that it is all one colour. The night sky looks like a black blanket. But if you took a trip to the North Pole, then you might see lots of colours in the sky!

Thousands of metres in the sky, light from the Sun bounces off the blanket of air around Earth known as the atmosphere. It makes waves and sheets of colour in the night sky. The northern lights look like waves of blue and green. They are brightest from December to March.

At the South Pole, you would see the southern lights. They are also waves of blue and green light. These lights appear above Antarctica. They glow most brightly from May to October.

The northern and southern lights are known as the *Aurorae*. They are like our planet's very own fireworks!

Let's Understand

Read the questions about *The Northern Lights.*
Put an ✖ next to the correct answer.

1. Why do the northern lights happen?

- ☐ We set off fireworks.
- ☐ Light bounces off the atmosphere.
- ☐ Nobody knows.

2. When are the northern lights most bright?

- ☐ May to June
- ☐ August
- ☐ December to March

3. When are the southern lights most bright?

- ☐ May to October
- ☐ December to March
- ☐ April

4. What colour are the northern and southern lights?

- ☐ red and gold
- ☐ blue and green
- ☐ silver

How did you go? Did you guess what the story would be about?

Fill in the diagram about the northern and southern lights.
Use words from the box.
Read how they are the same. Write how they are different.

North   December   South

May   October   March

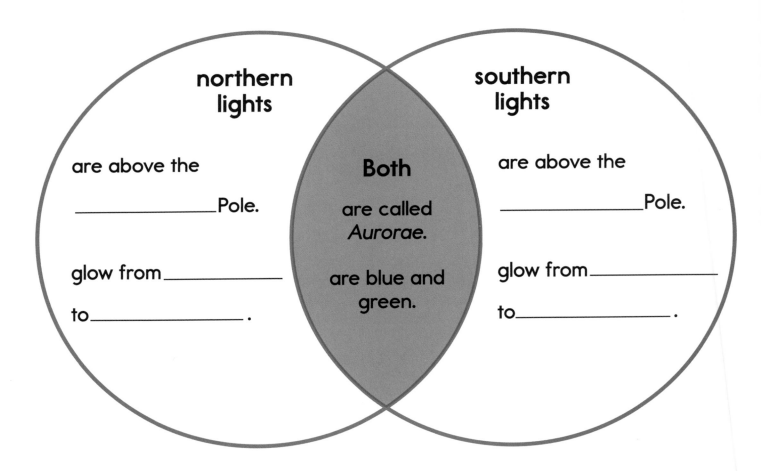

northern lights

are above the

_____Pole.

glow from_____

to_____ .

Both

are called *Aurorae.*

are blue and green.

southern lights

are above the

_____Pole.

glow from_____

to_____ .

Let's Compare

The northern lights happen thousands of metres up in the sky. That's much taller than we are! How tall are you? Ask a friend to measure you.

WOW! That is bigger than me or you!

I am _____ centimetres tall.

Draw something that is taller than you.
Draw something that is shorter than you.
Label your pictures.

Taller than me	Shorter than me
_____	_____
- - - - - - - - - - - -	- - - - - - - - - - - -
_____	_____

Let's Learn
Compound Words

Some words are made with two words.
Words that are made with two words are **compound words**.

Butterfly is a **compound** word.

butter + fly = butterfly

Write the **compound** words.
Find the matching stickers.

sun + shine

_____

- - - - - - - - - - - - - - - - -

_____

snow + man

_____

- - - - - - - - - - - - - - - - -

_____

lamp + post

_____

- - - - - - - - - - - - - - - - -

_____

bed + room

_____

- - - - - - - - - - - - - - - - -

_____

Sisters

Anna and Elsa are sisters.

Elsa likes to be neat.
Anna likes to be messy.

Anna likes playing outdoors.
Elsa likes reading indoors.

But Anna and Elsa both like to make snowmen!

Think about Anna and Elsa.
Write how they are alike and how they are different.

Anna likes	They both like	Elsa likes

Anna and Elsa find some papers tucked inside a book.
'It's a play about you and I when we were little,' says Elsa.
'Let's read it and act it out!' cries Anna.

Do You Want to Build a Snowman?

Characters:  **Elsa**  **Anna**

Elsa: It's time for bed, Anna.

Anna: I can't sleep. Let's do something fun!

Elsa: What would you like to do?

Anna: Do you want to build a snowman?

Elsa: (laughs) All right! (Elsa waves her hand. It begins to snow.)

Anna: First, we need to make a big, round body. (They roll a big snowball.)

Elsa: Now we're going to need a head. (They roll a smaller snowball.)

Anna: We can use these twigs for arms! (They stick in the twigs.)

Elsa: And these rocks make good eyes. (They put in the eyes.) Hmm. Something is missing.

Anna: (claps) I know! He needs a big, carroty nose!

Elsa: (laughs) Yes! That is just what he needs, Anna!

Let's Retell the Story

Cut out the puppets. Tape each puppet to a spoon.
Use the puppets to retell **Do You Want to Build a Snowman?**
Make your voice sound like the characters in the play.

© Disney

© Disney

© Disney

© Disney

Let's Write

Write something that Anna and Elsa might say to each other.

A Birthday Mystery

Anna was excited about Kristoff's birthday party. Elsa had made Kristoff an ice sculpture! It sparkled in the sun.

Anna had baked a cake. 'It's your favourite!' she told Kristoff. Everyone went to eat cake and other yummy birthday food.

Later, it was time for Kristoff to open his birthday presents. Sven gave him a carrot. Olaf picked him a bunch of flowers. Next, Elsa went to give Kristoff his ice sculpture. But it was nowhere to be found!

Where did the sculpture go? Everyone looked high and low.

'I can't find it,' said Olaf. 'All I see is this puddle of water.'

'Of course!' said Kristoff. 'The sun was shining through the window. The sculpture must have melted!'

Elsa waved her hand and made another beautiful sculpture!
'Happy birthday, Kristoff!' everyone said.

Let's Understand

Read the questions about **A Birthday Mystery.**
Put an **✗** next to the correct answer.

1. **What did Anna make for Kristoff?**

   ☐ a cake

   ☐ a sculpture

   ☐ a card

2. **What went missing from the party?**

   ☐ three cupcakes

   ☐ a hat

   ☐ an ice sculpture

3. **What clue did Olaf see?**

   ☐ crumbs

   ☐ a puddle

   ☐ footprints

4. **What happened to the missing thing?**

   ☐ It melted in the sun.

   ☐ It was stolen.

   ☐ It went for a walk.

Think about the story, *A Birthday Mystery.*
What is Elsa's problem?

_____

- -

_____

_____

- -

_____

Draw a picture that shows how Elsa solved the problem.

Let's Write

Draw a picture of something you lost.
Complete the sentences.

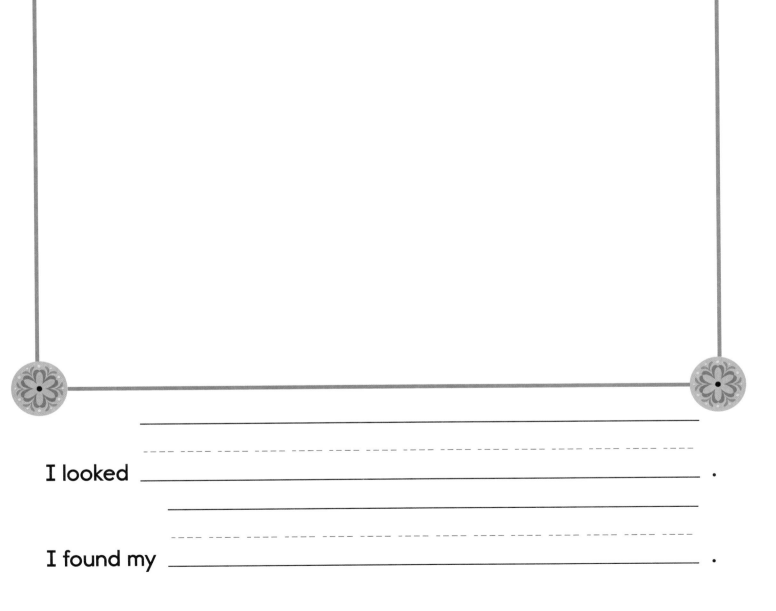

_____

- -

I looked _____ .

_____

- -

I found my _____ .

Let's Learn Vocabulary

Read each sentence.
Write a word from the box that has the same meaning.
Find the matching sticker.

race	fun	jump	pretty

1. This word means *very nice to look at.*

   _____

2. This word means *to run very fast.*

   _____

3. This word means *to have a good time.*

   _____

4. This word means *to spring into the air.*

   _____

The Great Idea

Olaf loved the summertime. He loved to sit on the beach and play in the park. But Olaf was a snowman. A snowman could not stay out in the sun. He would melt if he got too warm!

Elsa had a great idea. She made a small, cold cloud above Olaf's head. It would keep him cool when the day got warm.

Olaf was so happy. He could now spend time in the sunshine!

Put an ✖ next to the correct answer.

1. What is Olaf's problem?

☐ He liked the beach.

☐ He would melt if he got too hot.

☐ He didn't do his homework.

---

2. How did Elsa solve the problem?

☐ She created a cold cloud.

☐ She gave Olaf some ice.

☐ She took Olaf to the mountains.

Here's a poem about summer.

Summertime

You know, winter is fun
But when it's all done
Out comes the sun!
It's time for summer.

Birds sweetly sing
And they flutter their wings.
Want to play on the swings?
Come on, it's summer!

Doesn't it feel so grand
To lie on the sand?
There's a cool drink in my hand
In the summer.

When the warm breeze blows
The grass quivers and grows.
It tickles my nose
Every summer!

Oh, summer is great!
Every year I can't wait.
I'm counting the dates
Until summer!

Read the poem again following the instructions below.
Mark off each instruction with an ✘ when you're finished.

☐ **Make your voice excited when you see !**

☐ **Make your voice go up when you see ?**

☐ **Read the poem fast.**

☐ **Read the poem slow.**

☐ **Read the poem taking turns with a friend.**

You read one line.
Your friend reads the next line.

☐ **Use spoons to keep a beat.**

Hit two spoons together as you read.
Tap out the rhythm in the poem.

Let's Write

Help write a story about two sisters.
One sister is named Elsa.
Write the name of the other sister.

_____

- -

_____

There is a reindeer in the story.
What colour is the reindeer?

_____

- -

_____

Write the reindeer's name.

_____

- -

_____

Now pull out the next page. Fold it to make a book. Fill in the
blanks where you see them. Colour the pictures.

Who Lives on the Mountain?

Who lives on the north mountain? Elsa and her sister, _____, are going to find out.

They reach the top of the mountain. It is not scary at all! No big snow monster lives on the mountain. A friendly snowman lives there instead.

'Hi!' says the snowman. 'I'm Olaf. I like warm hugs.'

They all go back down the mountain.

4

© Disney

© D

Kristoff and his reindeer, _____, go with the sisters. They will help them on the trip. The reindeer's fur is warm and _____.

'I heard that a scary snow monster lives on the mountain,' says Kristoff. 'He is big and covered in sharp ice. You can hear him roar when the wind blows.'

Elsa and _____ shiver. 'I hope you are wrong,' says Elsa.

Anna looks over at Elsa.

'You love to read, don't you, Elsa?' she says. 'Ever since we were little girls, you loved to be indoors with a good book.'

Elsa smiles. 'And you were always much happier galloping around on your pony!'

'Even though we are sisters, we have always been so different,' says Anna.

'Yes,' says Elsa. 'But we have lots of things in common. Now you love to read, too!'

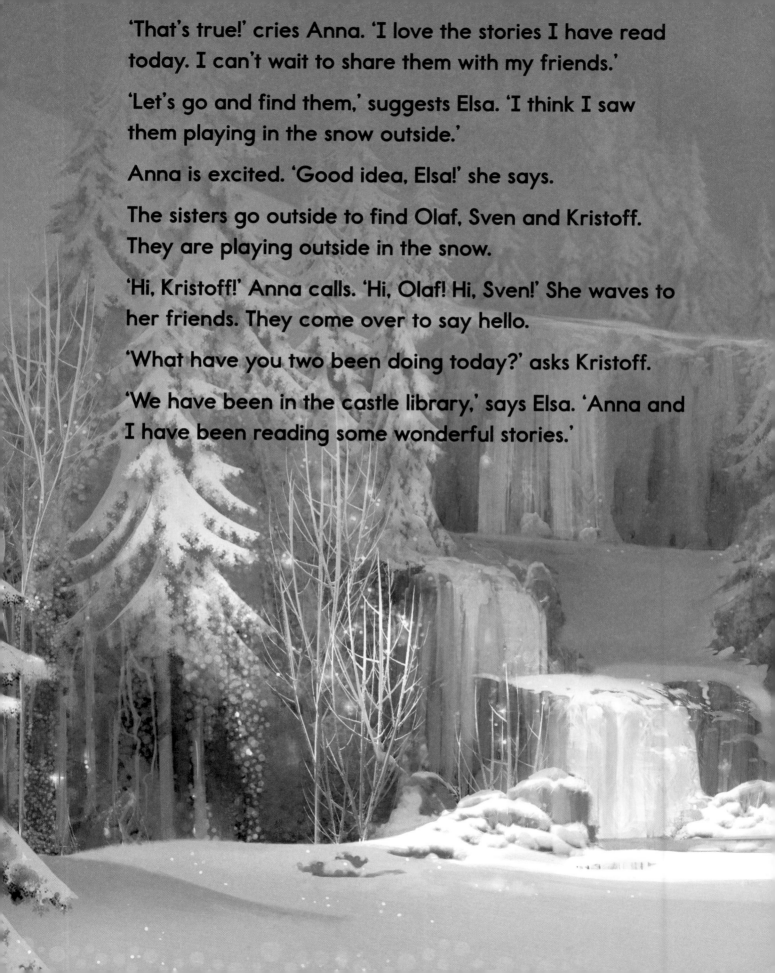

'That's true!' cries Anna. 'I love the stories I have read today. I can't wait to share them with my friends.'

'Let's go and find them,' suggests Elsa. 'I think I saw them playing in the snow outside.'

Anna is excited. 'Good idea, Elsa!' she says.

The sisters go outside to find Olaf, Sven and Kristoff. They are playing outside in the snow.

'Hi, Kristoff!' Anna calls. 'Hi, Olaf! Hi, Sven!' She waves to her friends. They come over to say hello.

'What have you two been doing today?' asks Kristoff.

'We have been in the castle library,' says Elsa. 'Anna and I have been reading some wonderful stories.'

Olaf gasps. 'I just *love* stories!' he says. 'I love them nearly as much as I love the sunshine and the summertime!' Sven nods his head. He loves stories, too.

Elsa laughs. 'Well, then, you're going to love what Anna has planned! She has brought lots of stories to share with all of us.'

Everyone is excited. What a perfect way to end a perfect day!

Answer Keys

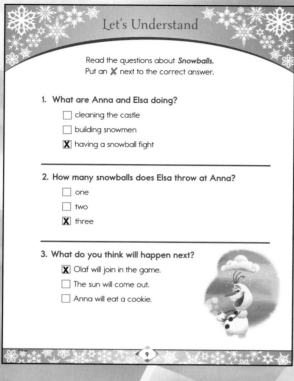

Let's Understand

Read the questions about *Snowballs.*
Put an ✗ next to the correct answer.

1. What are Anna and Elsa doing?
   - [ ] cleaning the castle
   - [ ] building snowmen
   - [✗] having a snowball fight

2. How many snowballs does Elsa throw at Anna?
   - [ ] one
   - [ ] two
   - [✗] three

3. What do you think will happen next?
   - [✗] Olaf will join in the game.
   - [ ] The sun will come out.
   - [ ] Anna will eat a cookie.

9

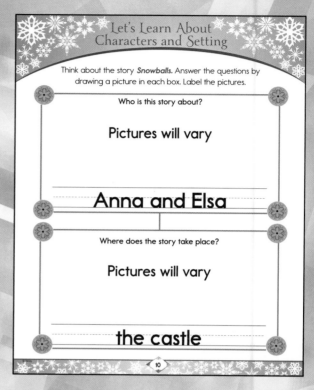

Let's Learn About Characters and Setting

Think about the story *Snowballs.* Answer the questions by drawing a picture in each box. Label the pictures.

Who is this story about?

Pictures will vary

Anna and Elsa

Where does the story take place?

Pictures will vary

the castle

10

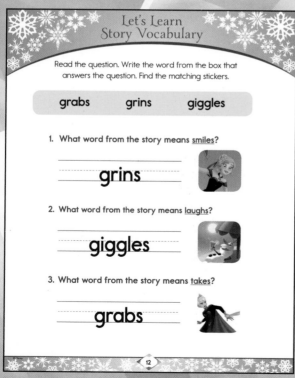

Let's Learn Story Vocabulary

Read the question. Write the word from the box that answers the question. Find the matching stickers.

grabs   grins   giggles

1. What word from the story means <u>smiles</u>?

   grins

2. What word from the story means <u>laughs</u>?

   giggles

3. What word from the story means <u>takes</u>?

   grabs

12

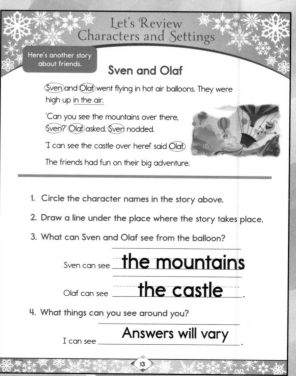

Let's Review Characters and Settings

Here's another story about friends.

Sven and Olaf

(Sven) and (Olaf) went flying in hot air balloons. They were high up <u>in the air.</u>

'Can you see the mountains over there, (Sven)?' (Olaf) asked. (Sven) nodded.

'I can see the castle over here!' said (Olaf)

The friends had fun on their big adventure.

1. Circle the character names in the story above.
2. Draw a line under the place where the story takes place.
3. What can Sven and Olaf see from the balloon?

   Sven can see **the mountains**

   Olaf can see **the castle**.

4. What things can you see around you?

   I can see **Answers will vary**.

13

Answer Keys

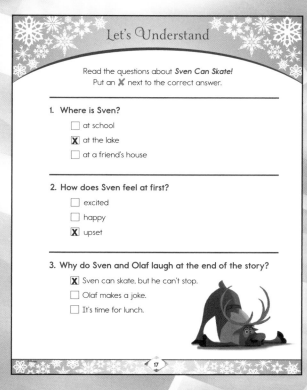

Let's Understand

Read the questions about *Sven Can Skate!*
Put an ✗ next to the correct answer.

1. Where is Sven?
   - ☐ at school
   - ☒ at the lake
   - ☐ at a friend's house

2. How does Sven feel at first?
   - ☐ excited
   - ☐ happy
   - ☒ upset

3. Why do Sven and Olaf laugh at the end of the story?
   - ☒ Sven can skate, but he can't stop.
   - ☐ Olaf makes a joke.
   - ☐ It's time for lunch.

17

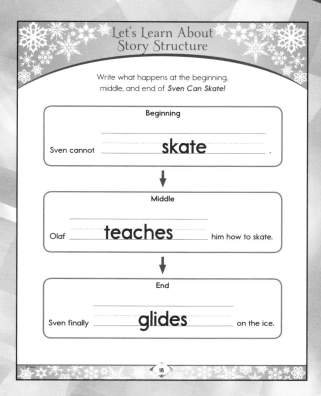

Let's Learn About Story Structure

Write what happens at the beginning, middle, and end of *Sven Can Skate!*

Beginning

Sven cannot ___**skate**___.

↓

Middle

Olaf ___**teaches**___ him how to skate.

↓

End

Sven finally ___**glides**___ on the ice.

18

Let's Learn Antonyms

Some words have opposite meanings.
Words that have opposite meanings are called **antonyms**.
Happy and sad are **antonyms**.
Use a word from the box to write the **antonym**.
Find the matching stickers.

under	cold	night

1. hot

   ___**cold**___

2. over

   ___**under**___

3. day

   ___**night**___

20

67

Answer Keys

Let's Understand

Read the questions about *A New Reindeer Friend.*
Put an ✗ next to the correct answer.

1. **Where did Anna and Elsa go?**
   - ☐ to the shops
   - ☐ to the moon
   - ☒ to the mountains

2. **What did they find?**
   - ☒ a baby reindeer
   - ☐ a snowman
   - ☐ cookies

3. **Who pulled the reindeer to safety?**
   - ☐ Anna
   - ☒ Elsa and Olaf
   - ☐ Sven

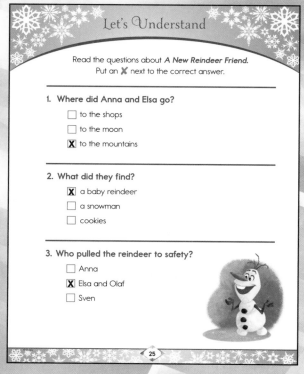

25

Let's Learn About Story Sequence

Find the stickers for *A New Reindeer Friend.*
Put them in the right order.
Use the stickers to retell the story.

First

Next

Last

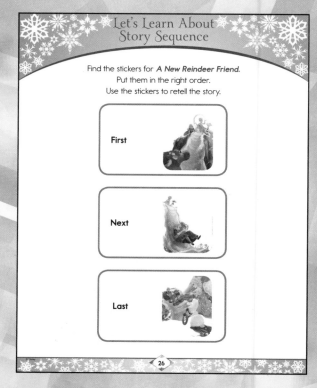

26

Let's Learn Synonyms

Some words mean the same thing.
Words that mean the same thing are called **synonyms**.
Big and large are **synonyms**.
Use a word from the box to write the **synonym**.
Find the matching stickers.

| afraid | glad | angry |

1. mad

   angry

2. scared

   afraid

3. happy

   glad

28

Answer Keys

Let's Review Story Sequence

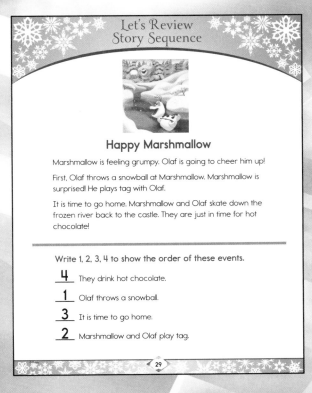

Happy Marshmallow

Marshmallow is feeling grumpy. Olaf is going to cheer him up!

First, Olaf throws a snowball at Marshmallow. Marshmallow is surprised! He plays tag with Olaf.

It is time to go home. Marshmallow and Olaf skate down the frozen river back to the castle. They are just in time for hot chocolate!

Write 1, 2, 3, 4 to show the order of these events.

4 They drink hot chocolate.

1 Olaf throws a snowball.

3 It is time to go home.

2 Marshmallow and Olaf play tag.

29

Let's Learn About Diagrams

A ship is made of many parts. Look at the diagram. Answer the questions.

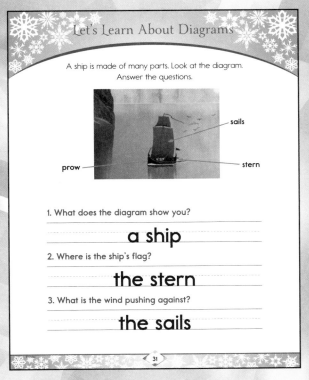

sails

prow

stern

1. What does the diagram show you?

a ship

2. Where is the ship's flag?

the stern

3. What is the wind pushing against?

the sails

31

Let's Understand

Read the questions about *Kronborg Castle.*
Put an ✗ next to the correct answer.

1. Kronborg Castle is _____.
   - **X** very old
   - ☐ make-believe
   - ☐ very new

2. The castle is built out of _____.
   - ☐ cake and chips
   - **X** stone
   - ☐ bricks

3. The castle was once damaged by _____.
   - ☐ an earthquake
   - ☐ a storm
   - **X** a fire

4. Today, Kronborg Castle is _____.
   - **X** a museum
   - ☐ where the King of Denmark lives
   - ☐ no longer standing

33

Let's Understand

Think about the story *Kronborg Castle.*
Complete the sentences.
Draw a picture to go with each sentence.

Pictures will vary

The castle has many **towers**.

Pictures will vary

There is a high **wall** around the castle.

34

69

Answer Keys

Let's Review

Draw a line to match words that are **antonyms**.

hot — cold
sad — happy
over — under
night — day

Draw a line to match words that are **synonyms**.

afraid — scared
mad — angry
glad — happy
cold — chilly

Let's Review
Cause and Effect

The Bees and the Coconut

Olaf was on a sunny holiday. He had a nap under a big coconut tree. When he woke up, he saw a big, shiny coconut high up in the tree.

'I want to pick that coconut for Queen Elsa.' He climbed up the tree trunk. He twisted the coconut in his hands. POP! Off came the coconut. Then he heard a buzzing noise. It was coming from the coconut!

'Oh dear!' said Olaf. 'It was not a coconut at all. It was a beehive!' The bees came out of the hive. They flew around Olaf's head. They sat on his nose.

'It's lucky I'm not afraid of bees,' Olaf said. 'They can't sting my carrot nose. But I will put the hive back into the tree. I can find another coconut to give to Queen Elsa!'

What did Olaf do?

He picked a coconut.

What happened?

It was a beehive.

Answer Keys

Let's Make Predictions

Anna is going to read *The Northern Lights.*

What do you think *The Northern Lights* will be about?

Answers will vary

Put an ✗ next to one thing you might learn about in *The Northern Lights.*

☐ Santa Claus
☒ lights in the northern sky
☐ a shop that sells lights
☐ stars

Now, let's read to find out!

41

Let's Understand

Read the questions about *The Northern Lights.*
Put an ✗ next to the correct answer.

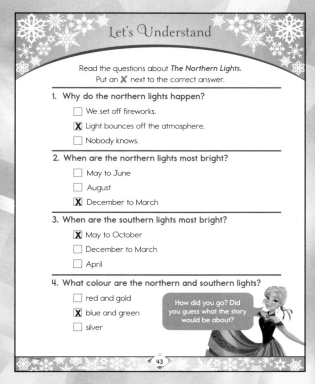

1. **Why do the northern lights happen?**
   ☐ We set off fireworks.
   ☒ Light bounces off the atmosphere.
   ☐ Nobody knows.

2. **When are the northern lights most bright?**
   ☐ May to June
   ☐ August
   ☒ December to March

3. **When are the southern lights most bright?**
   ☒ May to October
   ☐ December to March
   ☐ April

4. **What colour are the northern and southern lights?**
   ☐ red and gold
   ☒ blue and green
   ☐ silver

   > How did you go? Did you guess what the story would be about?

43

Let's Compare and Contrast

Fill in the diagram about the northern and southern lights.
Use words from the box.
Read how they are the same. Write how they are different.

North	December	South
May	October	March

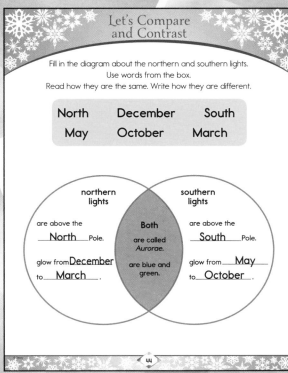

northern lights
are above the __North__ Pole.
glow from __December__ to __March__.

Both
are called *Aurorae.*
are blue and green.

southern lights
are above the __South__ Pole.
glow from __May__ to __October__.

44

Let's Compare

The northern lights happen thousands of metres up in the sky. That's much taller than we are!
How tall are you? Ask a friend to measure you.

> WOW! That is bigger than me or you!

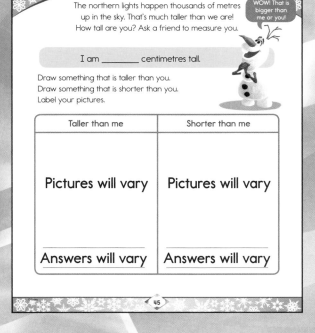

I am _____ centimetres tall.

Draw something that is taller than you.
Draw something that is shorter than you.
Label your pictures.

Taller than me	Shorter than me
Pictures will vary	Pictures will vary
Answers will vary	Answers will vary

45

Answer Keys

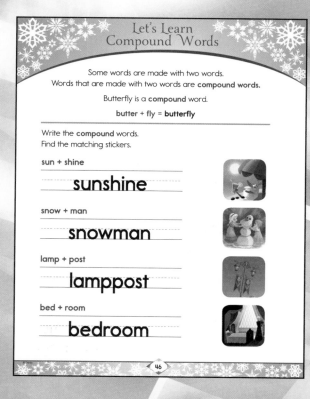

Let's Learn Compound Words

Some words are made with two words.
Words that are made with two words are **compound words**.

Butterfly is a **compound** word.

butter + fly = **butterfly**

Write the **compound** words.
Find the matching stickers.

sun + shine

sunshine

snow + man

snowman

lamp + post

lamppost

bed + room

bedroom

46

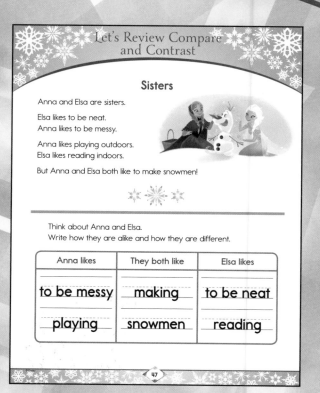

Let's Review Compare and Contrast

Sisters

Anna and Elsa are sisters.

Elsa likes to be neat.
Anna likes to be messy.

Anna likes playing outdoors.
Elsa likes reading indoors.

But Anna and Elsa both like to make snowmen!

✳ ❋ ✳

Think about Anna and Elsa.
Write how they are alike and how they are different.

Anna likes	They both like	Elsa likes
to be messy	making	to be neat
playing	snowmen	reading

47

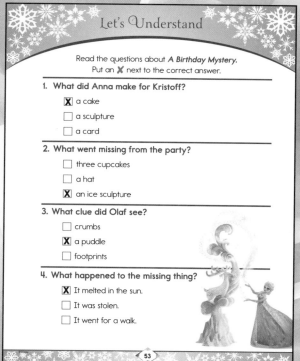

Let's Understand

Read the questions about *A Birthday Mystery*.
Put an ✗ next to the correct answer.

1. What did Anna make for Kristoff?
   - [✗] a cake
   - [ ] a sculpture
   - [ ] a card

2. What went missing from the party?
   - [ ] three cupcakes
   - [ ] a hat
   - [✗] an ice sculpture

3. What clue did Olaf see?
   - [ ] crumbs
   - [✗] a puddle
   - [ ] footprints

4. What happened to the missing thing?
   - [✗] It melted in the sun.
   - [ ] It was stolen.
   - [ ] It went for a walk.

53

Let's Learn About Problem and Solution

Think about the story, *A Birthday Mystery*.
What is Elsa's problem?

Kristoff's gift is missing.

Draw a picture that shows how Elsa solved the problem.

Pictures will vary

54

72

Answer Keys

Let's Learn Vocabulary

Read each sentence.
Write a word from the box that has the same meaning.
Find the matching sticker.

race	fun	jump	pretty

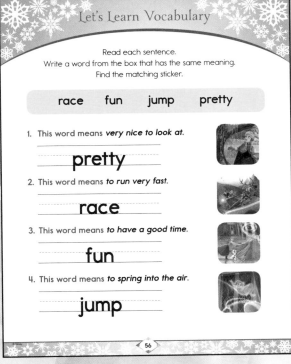

1. This word means *very nice to look at*.

   pretty

2. This word means *to run very fast*.

   race

3. This word means *to have a good time*.

   fun

4. This word means *to spring into the air*.

   jump

56

Let's Review
Problem and Solution

The Great Idea

Olaf loved the summertime. He loved to sit on the beach and play in the park. But Olaf was a snowman. A snowman could not stay out in the sun. He would melt if he got too warm!

Elsa had a great idea. She made a small, cold cloud above Olaf's head. It would keep him cool when the day got warm.

Olaf was so happy. He could now spend time in the sunshine!

Put an ✗ next to the correct answer.

1. **What is Olaf's problem?**
   - ☐ He liked the beach.
   - ☒ He would melt if he got too hot.
   - ☐ He didn't do his homework.

2. **How did Elsa solve the problem?**
   - ☒ She created a cold cloud.
   - ☐ She gave Olaf some ice.
   - ☐ She took Olaf to the mountains.

57

Let's Write

Help write a story about two sisters.
One sister is named Elsa.
Write the name of the other sister.

Anna

There is a reindeer in the story.
What colour is the reindeer?

brown

Write the reindeer's name.

Sven

Now pull out the next page. Fold it to make a book. Fill in the blanks where you see them. Colour the pictures.

60

I can read ...

Make-believe
stories

True stories

Poems

Plays

Put a snowflake
sticker next to
the things that
you can do!

I can ...

Describe characters
in a story

Describe a story's
setting

Describe what happens
in the beginning, middle
and end of a story

Answer questions
about stories

Make connections to
my own experiences

Retell stories

Predict what might
happen next in a story

I can ...

Name story events that cause other things to happen

Describe how a problem in a story was solved

Understand how things in a story are alike and different

GREAT JOB!

I can read ...

Story words

skate	race
fun	grins
castle	grabs
snowball	

Compound words

butterfly	sunshine
snowman	lamppost

Synonyms

afraid	scared
glad	happy
chilly	cold
angry	mad

Antonyms

hot	cold
over	under
day	night
happy	sad

How does your child learn?

Research shows that children benefit from a wide range of learning activities. Here are a few exercises you can do together to improve your child's reading comprehension.

Point out key words that help order and sequence.

As you complete simple projects and activities together, draw attention to words that suggest a specific order. For example, if you bake cupcakes, ask:

What do we need to do first?

What do we need to do next?

What do we need to do last?

Compare and contrast events together.

Share memorable experiences to make comparisons, such as the time you got a favourite stuffed toy. Share specific details about the experience and how you felt, and then ask your child to think about a similar experience.

In your conversation, draw attention to how the two experiences are the same, and how they are different. For example:

Parent: When I was your age, I got a teddy bear for my birthday. It was fluffy and brown. It made me very happy.

Child: I just got a dog for my birthday. It's very soft and black. I love it!

Develop healthy reading habits.

To encourage your child to read whenever possible, visit book spaces such as libraries and bookshops together often. Creating a book log can help promote a sense of achievement and keep track of what books your child has read and is currently reading. There are many different kinds of books for you to experience together: silly books, poetry books, information books, picture books, chapter books, craft books and so on. As your child's reading progresses, you will find that they develop their own taste in books that will affect what they choose to read. Daily independent reading time will help nurture your child's healthy reading habits.

Make story maps.

After reading a familiar story, create a story map together. Talk about what happened in the beginning, middle and end of the story. Then, on three long, narrow sheets of paper, encourage your child to draw pictures to map those events and write sentences about each part. Where appropriate, add character names and places. When you are both happy with the information gathered, tape the sheets of paper together at each edge to make a 'map', as shown below. Use the story map to retell the story.

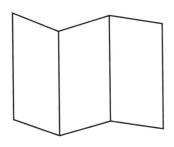

Could this happen?

Some stories sound real but are not, and some stories sound make-believe, but are in fact real. Browse through some favourite picture books together, using sticky notes to mark events in the story that could really happen. You can talk together about how some writers like to use both real-life and make-believe parts in a story. Discuss how this can make the story events even more fun and easier to relate to.

Make up new endings.

After reading a favourite story together, talk about ways to change the ending. What would happen if the character did something differently? What would happen if a new character came along? What would happen if you changed how the story problem was solved? Encourage your child to write down his or her ideas.

Share your thoughts before, during and after you read.

Sharing personal reflections can enhance the reading experience. For example, before you read a nonfiction book aloud, take some time to talk about what you and your child know about the topic. If the book is about a frog, share a few things you already know before reading. After finishing the book, share two things you have learned about frogs.

Talk about the books you read together to extend the reading experience. What were your favourite parts? What did you find funny? What parts were confusing? How did certain characters make you feel? What did different parts of the story remind you of? These brief conversations will help your child develop confidence in sharing his or her own questions, opinions and reflections about a story or book.

CONGRATULATIONS!

_____
(Name)

has completed the Disney Learning Workbook:

HOW TO READ
AND UNDERSTAND

Presented on

_____
(Date)

_____
(Parent's Signature)

Disney
FROZEN